Half hat

Two shoes,
each half

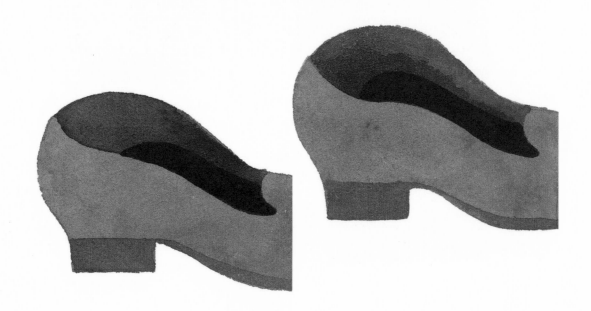

In the Half Room

Carson Ellis

Half chair

Half table

Half cat

Half a window

Half a door

Half a rug on half a floor

The light of the half moon

shines down on the half room.

*Half flowers
in half a vase*

Half a book

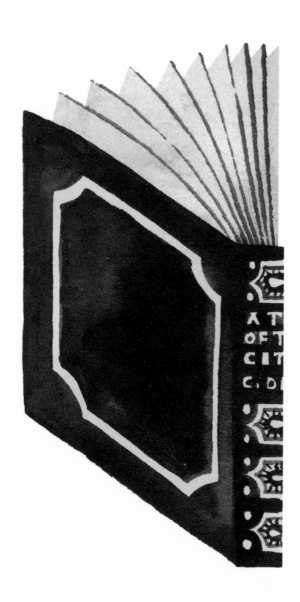

Half a face

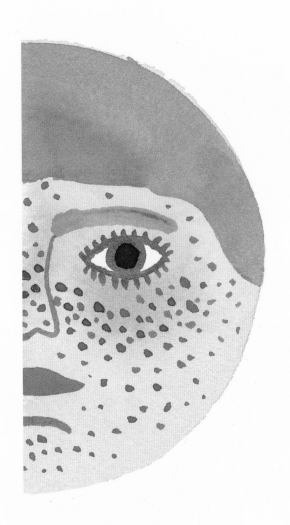

Half a moon

in a half-moon phase

Half a rug on half a floor

Half a knock on half a door

Half a face

you've seen before.

SHOOOOOP

Half lamp
Half light

Two half shoes
in the half
moonlight

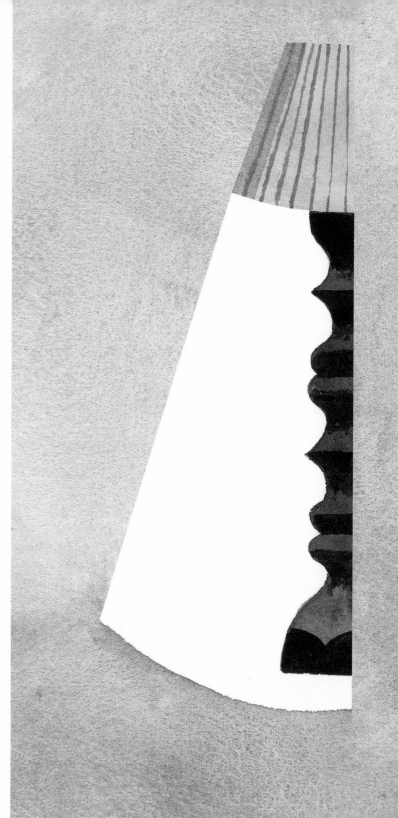

Half a rug on half a floor

Half a cat is at the door.

Two half cats
in a half-cat fight

Two half cats asleep

Good night!

The End

This book is for my son, Milo. He gave me the idea for it and he cheered me on while I made it, even though he's not sure about the ending. This book is also for my cats, past and present: Couscous, Kip, Alice, China, Albert, Fortinbras, Window and Moony. Muses, all.

First published 2020 by Walker Books Ltd, 87 Vauxhall Walk, London SE11 5HJ • This edition published 2021 • © 2020 Carson Ellis • The right of Carson Ellis to be identified as the author and illustrator of this work has been asserted by her in accordance with the Copyright, Designs and Patents Act 1988 This book has been typeset in Normande Standard Italic • Printed in China • All rights reserved. No part of this book may be reproduced, transmitted or stored in an information retrieval system in any form or by any means, graphic, electronic or mechanical, including photocopying, taping and recording, without prior written permission from the publisher. • British Library Cataloguing in Publication Data: a catalogue record for this book is available from the British Library • ISBN 978-1-4063-9983-7 • www.walker.co.uk • 10 9 8 7 6 5 4 3 2 1